Dedalus Orig

The Romeo & Juliet Killers

Xavier Leret was born and bred in Bristol.

He has written and directed two feature films and numerous theatre productions. He now lives in a small village not far from Bishops Stortford.

The Romeo & Juliet Killers is his first novel.

Xavier Leret

The Romeo & Juliet Killers

Dedalus

Supported using public funding by
ARTS COUNCIL ENGLAND

Published in the UK by Dedalus Limited,
24-26, St Judith's Lane, Sawtry, Cambs, PE28 5XE
email: info@dedalusbooks.com
www.dedalusbooks.com

ISBN printed book 978 1 910213 18 6
ISBN ebook 978 1 910213 28 5

Dedalus is distributed in the USA & Canada by SCB Distributors,
15608 South New Century Drive, Gardena, CA 90248
email: info@scbdistributors.com   web: www.scbdistributors.com

Dedalus is distributed in Australia by Peribo Pty Ltd.
58, Beaumont Road, Mount Kuring-gai, N.S.W. 2080
email: info@peribo.com.au

First published by Dedalus in 2015

The Romeo & Juliet Killers copyright © *Xavier Leret 2015*

The right of Xavier Leret to be identified as the author of this work has been asserted by him in accordance with the Copyright, Designs and Patents Act, 1988.

Printed in Finland by Bookwell
Typeset by Marie Lane

This book is sold subject to the condition that it shall not, by way of trade or otherwise, be lent, resold, hired out or otherwise circulated without the publisher's prior consent in any form of binding or cover other than that in which it is published and without a similar condition including this condition being imposed on the subsequent purchaser.

A C.I.P. listing for this book is available on request.

For Sharon

"The latter contemplated the carnage (fragments of red flesh in the prairie, yellow flowers, men in black suits), sighed gently and turned around to his companion, saying, 'it's a moral duty, John'."

Michel Houellebecq

The Possibility of An Island

Act I

1

He was on his way home from school, walking with his head down, his sports holdall slung over his shoulder and he was terrified. A letter was going to be arriving the very next morning that would throw his parents into a puritanical fury. A teacher at his Catholic Free School had caught him watching a filthy movie on a friend's mobile phone.

Some parents might laugh off such lurid transgressions, perhaps even celebrate the sexual awakening of their sons. Many of the parents of his pals, he was sure, would do just that. But not his. Not in a month of Sundays. His parents being religiously strict in the most steadfast sense. His pals all had mobile phones and game consoles and their own computers in their rooms, and would regularly swap just about anything personal across innumerable social networking platforms. Many of them also seemed to have vast collections of dirty movies on their phones, some of which involved themselves, well that's what they claim. He wasn't allowed none of these. His mum was particularly disparaging of mobile phones and the internet claiming that they are like the many heads of the beast as chronicled by St John The Apostle in the Apocalypse, and would often argue that he was simply not old enough to withstand such temptations. His dad would rant on too, about the dissolute ravages of contemporary society and modern life.

But worse than this was that now he felt raw with shame,

wishing that he was stronger, better able to fight temptation, better able to understand his own body, knowing only too well, and indeed, fearing what his parents might say about his sexual awakenings, a topic he had never once dared to discuss with them, and an issue of his development they had never once raised with him. Were it not for the movies that he watched during his lunchtimes he would be entirely in the dark and out on a limb as to how to deal with girls and, more specifically, the passions that were raging within him. With his friends, in the playground, he achieved not just camaraderie but a sense that what he was experiencing was normal.

He walked and looked at the houses to either side of him and wondered what happened behind the windows, whether all family life was the same as his family life, whether their lives were populated by shouts and screams, visions, scourges, blood, demons, eternal damnation.

He wanted to pray for an end to his torment and some heavenly reprieve before the morning, but he didn't know how to, his problem being that he just couldn't believe, an unfortunate failure of his nurturing and not one that he could in any way explain. If only he did believe, life for him would be so much simpler. There certainly wouldn't be any letters home from school. On one level he sort of felt the presence of an alternative spiritual reality populated by the Trinity – Father, Son, Holy Ghost – saints, angels, cherubs and all the rest of them – it was, considering his home life, difficult for him not to. At the same time, however, his internal voice whispered that none of it was true. And as he walked that internal voice was working overtime, reeling off an angry monologue about how unfortunate he was, and how cruel life had been to him for giving him the parents that he had, when it suddenly fell silent. Just up ahead of him, slap bang in the middle of the pavement, blocking his way, stood a girl, his age or thereabouts, in a short skirt with bare legs, her figure tall and slender, her hair short, spiked and fiery red, her eyes like emeralds. A small silver handbag was slung over her shoulder and she was wearing a T-shirt with the words, *Heaven Sent*, embossed in gold across her young breasts.

She pretended not to see him, keeping her gaze on something way off down the street, but when he didn't move she scowled and said, "Fuck off".

He coughed, said, "Sorry," turned and, feeling that he was trapped in clothes two sizes too small for him, began to walk away.

"Wait," she called.

He stopped and turned.

"D'you's gone red," she said.

"Have I?"

"Yah."

Afraid of the silence he quickly said the first thing that popped into his mind, fluffing the natural beat of the conversation by swallowing the very first word of his sentence. "Wh-at school do you go to?"

The question made her blink. "School?" she said, which in her thick Bristolian accent, sounded more like scawl.

"Yeah," he said.

"I don't go a scawl."

"You don't?"

"Nah."

"How come?"

"Taint no scawl that wants I." The light in her eyes flinched. "Etz a fucker," she added, off-the-cuff-like. She took a pack of ten Marlboro Silvers out of her small handbag, put a cigarette to her lips and just before she lit it said, "Whir d'you goes?"

"Bart's," he answered.

She took a deep drag of her cigarette, blew out a shaft of smoke and nodded seriously, like she was aware of the esteemed holiness of the institution and felt nothing but sympathy for him for having to experience it.

"My name's Franky," he said. "What's yours?"

Her eyes squinted because the sun was behind him. "Daizee," she said.

"That's a nice name," he said softly.

She looked at him like she'd heard that before. "Ez et?"

"Yeah, it's a summer name, like the flower."

She laughed and put up her hand to block out the sun. Her eyes narrowed. "What, d'you's a poet?"

He shrugged his shoulders and did his best to appear relaxed, though deep down he wished he hadn't said it, not that he didn't write poetry because he did, it was just something that he kept to himself, hidden away in an exercise book under his bed, at home.

"Well, what can I do for d'you's then thur Mistur Shakespeares?"

"I'm going to get a coke, Daizee. Do you want one?"

Franky heard music. Her hips began to hustle. "A coke?" she said.

He couldn't help but smile as he watched her do a little jig. The movement of her hips making her pert breasts sway. "Yeah," he said.

"I don't jus go with any old cock, I'm not that sort of… D'you's got cash?"

Now Franky had managed to save two-days dinner money, which he planned to spend that weekend at the church youth club. Fasting to save was his parent's idea.

"I got meez a righteous feeling bout d'you's, ur lover,"

she said with a wink and took what little money he had, "like destiny jus poked I. Yah, tis troo," she grinned.

They went for a walk. He bought her an ice-cold coke and they sat in a park with swings, a slide, crushed in by houses, two tall-rooms high, with skylights scattered into the rooftops, the main road adjacent rammed with rush-hour traffic. And they chatted. And it was like a real date. She even took her phone out and snapped a photo of the two of them, cheek to cheek, said she'd text it to him, but Franky didn't have a phone, so she said, "No bother, I'll keeps it for d'you." A little while later she said, "Times up," so he said, "can we meet again?" And she said, "Yeah, sure fing, sweetz, I'z iz ooked all week but I can squeeze a bit of room for d'you's on Thursdi, so ow's about that?"

He nodded and said, "Ok."

She looked him in the eyes and smiled, a genuine, warm smile. "D'you's got yurself a pen then thur Mistur Shakespeares?"

"Yeah," he said softly.

"Well geez et ere then." She picked a piece of paper up from the floor, laid it on the bench and wrote her number down on it.

When Franky got home he put her number in the bible that his dad had given him as a child. His dad had inscribed it with, 'Don't loose your soul, Francis, whatever the world might offer.'

2

When she left him Daizee wandered into the town centre to a MacDonald's in the Union Gallery which was her favourite. She ordered herself a large chocolate thick-shake, sat by the window sucking on the straw and took her phone out to look at the photo of him.

There was a MacDonald's clown in a purple jumpsuit and a hooter of a red nose laughing, blowing up balloons, then letting them down whilst making a farting noise with his mouth. This little girl was laughing and laughing. All the clown had to do was make that farting noise and the girl would fall about in fits. Her laughter was totally infectious, bringing a smile to Daizee's face and before she knew it she was giggling along too.

Later, when she finished her shake she got up and walked pass the little girl and her mother. The girl smiled and waved. Daizee waved back. The mother looked up, smiled, but her eyes dropped when she saw who it is was her daughter was waving to. Daizee didn't mind a bit, she was happy. Once outside she lit a cigarette and walked past the shop windows. The mannequins were at play in the windows, walking hand in hand, lovers in swimwear.

3

Franky's day began as his life had the moment he first saw her. He sat bolt upright, smiling, went straight to his desk, took out his bible from the drawer and retrieved the scrap of paper on which she had scrawled her name and number, then lay down again and just stared at it.

The door to his bedroom flew open and his mum stormed into the room. He saw the edge of the screwed up letter poking out from her fist, and immediately felt sick.

"You have demeaned yourself".

"Mum –"

"Let me finish!" she said pronouncing every syllable as she was casting out a demon. "Have you no shame? Lusting over that filth. You corrupt yourself, just by looking at it."

"It wasn't like that –"

But she wasn't listening. "What am I going to tell your dad?"

His eyes were closed, his skin burning, his heart beating erratically. There was a barrage of words exploding inside his head, but none that he could harness into a coherent sentence, or utilise into a rational argument. And there was blistering shame. A searing disgust in himself and his body's unquenchable need for sexual fulfilment, that he could in no way control. There was no running away from it, it was always there, if not at the forefront of his mind, then in the shadows of it.

"And look!" she shouted, and held up the scrunched-up letter from the headmaster. "You've fallen so publicly. It is not just your shame, it's now mine and your dad's. Everyone will know. Each and every one of those parents, that called themselves Christians. I'll never be able to show my face at church again. We will have to go into school, and sit in front of your headmaster, that self important bank manager of a man, and share in this indignity. How am I supposed to tell your dad about this? What do I tell him?"

"I'm sorry mum."

"Sorry to whom? Me?"

Tears welled up in his eyes.

"Who you should be sorry to is our Father in heaven," she hissed. "He is disgusted by you, he is defiled by you."

He didn't know where to look so he looked at his feet which made him feel even more like a little boy.

"Why did you do it?"

"I don't know mum, a friend had it on his phone and everybody was looking at it."

"I knew that school was to blame."

"It's not school –"

"If it's not the school then what is it? Your friends? You must never trust your friends, Francis. All these people that live life as if their friends are the most important thing in the world, as if their friends are worth dying for. If your friends were going to all jump off a cliff, would you jump with them?"

He breathed out, he knew the speech, every cadence of it and he despised it.

"No of course you wouldn't. Your friends are nothing, they're worthless. There is nothing more important than Jesus Christ our Lord, our Saviour. It is he that you harm. He that sacrificed his life for you, you who are created in his image. It is that image that you defile."

He turned crimson with hatred, there were tears in his eyes, and he began to lie. "Please, mum, I'm sorry. It's never happened before, it'll never happen again. I didn't want to watch it, they made me, we were all chatting and then this phone came out. I was scared to not look. I was scared of what they might say. But it didn't mean anything. It was just films. That's all."

"I shall be going up to that school and I shall have to say something."

"Please mum, don't do that."

"What do you mean, don't do that? Do you think I have any choice? Do you think this letter is just politely informing me of your behaviour? They have requested my presence because they are at their wits end. And I am going to inform them of their woeful lack of discipline. What on earth are children doing with pornography on their phones? How on earth do they get such material? Are their parents aware, or is it that the parents are complicit in such depravity? Having met one or two of them, I don't doubt it. And they call themselves Catholics!"

"Mum, please."

"Shut up. Shut up, you've no right to speak to me. Can't you control yourself? Have we so let you down that you don't know how to behave?"

"It was just a film, mum."

"It was not just a film. It was pornography!"

Franky looked at his feet again, his shoulders were shaking, his head was in his hands.

She altered her line of attack, softened her tone. "If you were feeling these impulses, needing to see this material, why didn't you come and talk to me, or your dad about it? We would have been happy to discuss it. We are your parents, you can talk to us about anything. Anything at all. We could have told you about the dangerous nature of these films, how they compromise the viewer, how they corrupt."

She stopped talking and looked intently at him. "We are always here, your dad and I. We love you Francis. You do know that?"

That's what she always said when she was attacking him like this, "We love you Francis, you know that?" But he didn't know it. And he didn't know if he loved them. Not really loved them. Need them, yes, but love? He forced himself to nod.

4

Daizee was sitting on a park bench, wearing a pair of sunglasses to hide a swollen black eye and smoking a cigarette butt that she'd found discarded on the floor. Her black eye had bloomed in the early hours not long after picking up some guy called Kev, who paid her in crisp new notes. Drunk, wired on cocaine, and wobbling on precarious stilettos, she had stumbled, lost control of her feet and and slammed eye first into a lamp post. Right in front of a couple of lads who then accused Kev of hitting her. Before long it was all fists and kicks, then rolling around the floor and trying to bite chunks out of each other. Daizee just stood there screaming and cursing, and even tried to drag the lads off Kev, but when she heard sirens, she cut her losses and hobbled off into the shadows, her long limbs spindled and staggering on her pin heels.

Once she was sure that there was no one following her, she fished her phone from out of her jacket pocket and would have called a cab had the phone had any juice. It took her half an hour to hail a ride. Just as she was climbing into the car she realised that she had lost her bag somewhere along the line and had no way of paying to get home. After turning down her offer of a blow-job, the cabbie drove off.

The skies were clear, so it was cold. She had nothing on her legs, her short dress barely hid her wares, let alone kept the chill off. Because of her eye, and the drink, and her nose full of coke she couldn't see straight. Everything was a blur, the cars that sped past, the puddles of water in the street. Her head dropped back and she looked up to the light-polluted sky, screamed in frustration, threw off her shoes and began the four-mile hike back to Fishponds.

The birds had set about their hollering when finally she fell into her bed after having had to break into the building, which was none too hard because the lock had been kicked in that many times.

Everything, had been been in that bag, cash, debit cards, you name it. And those coins of Franky's that she'd been keeping for good luck. Not that they had bought her any.

Everything, except her phone, which she kept in a pocket so she could hear Marvin Gaye sing, "I want sexual healing," when somebody called. It always made the punters laugh.

Her head ached too much to be overly sentimental about all her stuff that was lost. More importantly, what with her eye being the way it was, she wouldn't be earning for a few days, because there was no way she could turn up at some client's hotel looking like a beaten housewife, or some common street-whore. The cruel irony being that a common street-whore is what she would have to be, whilst she waited for a new card to arrive. Either that or starve.

Sitting in the park she watched mothers chatting as their children played and found herself thinking about her mum. As the women gassed and fussed over their babies she wondered if Cristol had ever gassed and fussed over her, if ever she got stopped in Asda's by old women cooing over her pram, if ever she lay beside her '*babee*' with a look of wonder in her eyes.

"Nah, probably not."

Just over the road from the park, some other mothers were chatting outside a primary school which, quite randomly, because she hadn't thought of it before, reminded her of her last day of primary school. The class got up and did a special assembly and sang a song about believing is achieving. Daizee didn't know the lyrics, because she'd missed so much of the year, only being there that day because the school had sent the inspectors round to fetch her. All the other kids had their parents present but not her. At the end of the song they all got given a year book with their photos in, except that, because she'd never really shown up, there were no photos of her. Then she got put in a care home, was forced into a school for a year or two, so at least she could read.

She never saw Cristol again.

She flicked the butt away. There must be a reason she was thinking about Cristol. It can't just have been because she was feeling sorry for herself. Maybe something was wrong. Maybe she was feeling a connection with her, because mothers and daughters have that spiritual bond across multiple dimensions. She'd read about it once in a magazine.

Daizee hadn't been home since they moved her out and settled her into care. Not once. Didn't really know how to get there, if truth be told, though she had a good memory of what the old place looked like.

"Fuck et," she said to herself. "Taint got nutten else to do," and set off to find err muh.

5

When his mum told his dad about the dirty movie his dad was silent for a long time and then he said as cruelly as he could muster, "So, Deirdre, this is what you have done." Which was what he always said if Franky was in trouble. He would also say it when Franky had said something to offend him. His dad always blamed his mum and his mum always accepted the blame. Franky hated the way his dad would do that, but he hated the way his mum accepted it just as much. It always seemed to him that his dad would blame everyone else but himself for all the things that went wrong. Franky always thought that if his dad wanted to take charge of his upbringing then he should be around more. But he wasn't, which Franky also saw as a good thing as his dad could really loose his temper. It didn't matter where they might be, or with whom, his dad could just loose it, and when that happened everyone in the surrounding streets knew about it. So, as far as Franky was concerned it was far better that he wasn't around.

After a long and fretful silence his dad made his mum phone the school and request an immediate appointment, insisting that they were seen without delay. He did this without shouting, but his hands were shaking. It was only a matter of time.

His mum had tried to keep as calm a voice as she could to the school secretary, which was difficult, because his dad was pacing and hissing vitriol under his breath at her.

The walk into school was almost a run, yet his dad kept his temper until the headmaster handed Franky a leaflet and made him read from it. The leaflet was about how the Magisterium of the Church considers masturbation a gravely disordered action. It was then, just as Franky finished reading, that Franky's dad lost his temper, and not to defend Franky because of the degrading way in which he was being treated, but to attack the school's policy on sex education, most of which Franky was excluded from anyway, his parents believing that this pastoral role was theirs and theirs alone.

And true to form his dad shouted loud enough to be heard all over the school. Or at least that's how it seemed to Franky as he fought to hold back his tears. He couldn't look at any one in that room. His mum was beside his dad, nodding along like she was in support of him.

This crushed Franky. All through his secondary school years he had lived in a fear, not so much of them and what they might do to him at home, he could live with that. The thing that really scared him was how they might behave outside of the home. He never liked going anywhere with them. They were never discrete about their disapproval and they disapproved, it seemed to him, of just about everything.

Afterwards Franky stomped his way back home wishing that he was dead, or that they were somewhere miles behind him. But he couldn't get as far away from them as he needed to, because every time he made a sizeable distance between him and them, his dad shouted for him to slow down. And even across the distance he could hear his dad berating his mum, "It's all your fault, he's losing the faith, you're not teaching him, you're not doing enough to pass it on to him."

At home Franky tried to escape to his room, but his dad stopped him. "We need to have a talk about this morning. And about you."

"I don't want to."

"Oh the big boy doesn't want to talk?" mocked his dad. "Where was that individualism when your friends took you aside to watch that pornography? I don't think that was anywhere in sight. No, at that moment, Francis 'the individual' was just another boy with no mind of his own. Well, Francis, I didn't want to see your headmaster this morning, but I didn't have any choice in the matter, that die was caste."

"You didn't have to go."

His dad flicked the leaflet, that the head had given them, into Franky's face, the edge of it caught him just below the eye.

"I am your parent, Francis, of course I had to go. That is my responsibility."

"Please Peter," interrupted his mum.

"Be quiet, woman, if you knew how to control him then none of this would have happened. But no, here we are again, and I have to pick up the pieces."

"Peter, you're being too harsh on him."

"Enough, Deirdre!" shouted his dad. "I am not sure how we should deal with you Francis. We have done everything for you. We have gone without. I myself have sacrificed a great many things so that you can have everything that a child needs. Am I out every night with my friends? Am I a drunkard? You don't know how easy you have it. Aren't you grateful? Because it seems to me that you're not."

Franky didn't answer instead he looked at his feet.

"Next time you feel these urges, Francis, you come to me, and we'll discuss it like gentlemen. I'm not just your father, I am a man. I understand something of what is happening to you. If you needed some guidance on how to control yourself, then why not ask me about it. But to allow yourself to be caught watching that material."

"I," started Franky, but he was cut off.

"Don't start an argument with me, Francis. Argument is not the answer. Argument won't help you address what you have done. What you have let into you life. What you have failed to control. You have simply shown us that you can't be trusted to behave decently. So I am left with no alternative than to treat you as a child. You must trust that I know best. I have been around a lot longer than you. Now, we are going to have to punish you. No, sin goes unpunished, Francis. From now on, until I deem fit, you must come home from school everyday and go straight to your room. But don't think for a moment that you are going to relax whilst you are in your room. You are in serious trouble. As the school has not provided you with a penance, then I shall. And I expect it done."

Franky stared at him.

"Now get out. Go to your room. You shall not leave it."

"What if I need to go to the toilet?"

"Then do it in your bed."

Act II

1

In the hours it took for Daizee to walk from Fishponds to Hartcliffe she went over a whole lot of stuff about her childhood that she hadn't thought about in a long time. Things like watching telly on her own whilst Cristol, and whoever it was she was doing at the time, were out. And waiting up for them like she was their mother. Falling asleep on the sofa before being woken up by their drunken laughter. And sometimes everyone was in good spirits, and sometimes they weren't.

When things were at their darkest she would put the smallest bit of herself in a doll. Her favourite doll that Cristol picked up for her once in an Oxfam shop. A mucky doll that had a slash across her rubber eye. This doll was the only one that Daizee kept because there was always someone hanging about who would want to fiddle with her toys and she didn't like that. But not with this doll because she would hide her away, under a floor board, in the bathroom, that creaked whenever a person walked over it. And inside the doll she would hide her own heart. In the room above, whispers would writhe and the room would creak and the bath that she slept in would rock. And dust would fall on the doll's head. Inside the doll Daizee locked herself away, scared, under the wood of that floor, like she was in her coffin.

It was late afternoon when finally she found herself on a cafe-crème-coloured council estate that looked like the one she'd grown up on. The tall block of flats dwarfing the small park with a piddly slide and swings. The grass long since worn away, the fence surrounding the play area still motley. Exactly as she'd left it. It was an island of the old life.

"Dean?" shrieked Cristol's voice before Daizee had even taken her finger from the buzzer.

Daizee looked at the little speaker. Even with the slight microphone crackle Cristol sounded like Cristol, a bit older perhaps, and a little more cackly and burnt out, but it was her mum, there was no doubt about it.

"Dean, whir the fuck d'you's been?"

Daizee bit her lip.

"Fucken answer I d'you cunt."

"Muh?"

"Who's that?"

"Daizee."

"Daizee?"

"Yeh, muh."

There was a long pause. Daizee lent against the door.

"What d'you wants?" said Cristol.

"Jus to say ello."

"D'you wants monee?"

Daizee breathed in deeply. "Nah," she said, "I was jus passin, muh."

"Jus passin? Throo Stanton Parks?"

"Yah."

"Fuck off."

"Tis troo."

There was another long pause. Daizee pictured her mum standing in the darkness of the corridor. It was bound to be dark, because it was always dark, because Cristol never got round to changing the bulb. It was probably the same burnt out bulb as the day she was taken into care.

"What d'you's doen back ere, Daizee? Thur's nutten for d'you's ere."

"D'you's wrong muh, thur's d'you."

Daizee looked at the buzzer through which her mum breathed heavily like that last cigarette might be the one to do her in. By the sounds of it she was standing with her face right close to it. She could be lent against the wall with her eyes closed in thought, her lips moving like she was having a conversation with herself. Daizee would often find her like that, lips muttering some internal argument with herself. "I don't want d'you's," said Cristol at last. "I don't want d'you's back. This taint no place for d'you's."

Daizee breathed out. She hadn't expected this. "Let I come up, muh. Et's been a long walk out ere. I jus needs to rest up and then I'll be on ur way."

This time there was a long cold silence. The damage, if there were to be any, had now been done and Cristol, Daizee could sense, knew it. Then Cristol said, sharply, "D'you promise d'you'll be gone?"

Daizee closed her eyes, breathed out. "I promise muh." The door buzzed open. She looked into the hall like she always used to do when she was little, to make sure that there was no one waiting for her. It all looked the same as when she left, even the same acidic smell of disinfectant. The coast was clear, so she crossed over to the lift, pressed the call button and waited. She heard gears change above and the gentle un-oiled squeak as the lift descended, and then a long pause after it clanged into position. The door opened and she saw her distorted reflection in the mirror opposite. Her black eye looked like it had been smudged on and her hair was a violent clown red.

It took Cristol a long time to answer the door and when she did Daizee was shocked. Silhouetted by the starved light behind her, Cristol was threadbare thin. Her front teeth were all missing. Her hair was scraggied and grey. Her eyes sunken and black beneath a canopy of crinkled skin on her forehead. But what shocked Daizee the most was that in that face that she hardly recognised, she saw herself.

Cristol sniffed, "What d'you's doen back ere gurl?"

"D'you not pleased to see I, muh?"

Cristol scowled. "Nah."

"I missed d'you muh. Why d'you not come and find I?"

"And do what?"

"I dunno. Jus see I. I would ave liked that."

"Would d'you?"

"Yeah, muh."

"I couldn't look after d'you. I was ne'er no good at et. D'you's ad more of a chance this way."

"D'you're ur muh, muh."

"Not no more."

They were standing in front of each other. Daizee taller than her mum who stood crooked and bent. She wanted Cristol to look her in the eyes, but Cristol didn't, she looked stubbornly ahead of herself. They stood for a good couple of minutes. Daizee watching her mum waiting for a look that she might recognise that would allow her to break the ice, but nothing came. Cristol was tiny and shrivelled and cold. Sometimes her lips moved, but most of the time she was still. Eventually Daizee says, "What about a cup of tea then muh?"

Cristol nodded but didn't look at Daizee. She turned then wandered back through the flat. "What appened to yur face?" She slurred over her shoulder, "Some fella punched d'you?"

"Nah, muh, et whir nutten like that."

"Nah? D'you looks cheap."

Daizee pulled her sunglasses down out of her hair and onto her eyes. "I'm doing alright," she said, closing the door behind her and immediately it was darker. As her eyes grew accustomed to the light she could make out that the floor of the flat was scattered with take-away boxes, bits of burgers and pizza, all covered in fur and almost luminously green. There was the strong smell of something rotting. She stepped carefully into the lounge in which there was only a sofa, an old telly on the floor, no carpet just exposed floor boards covered with cigarette butts, makeshift crack pipes, bits of metal gauze, used needles. By the sofa was an old tobacco tin in which had been thrown a filthy spoon and a blood-stained wad of dried cotton wool. It was much the same as she'd left it.

She wandered over to the kitchen. Cristol was standing looking out of the window. The sink was piled with dirty dishes. The doors to the shelves had been ripped off and the shelves were empty.

"I taint got no tea," said Cristol without looking at her.

Daizee shrugged her shoulders. "No matter."

"Whir d'you's livin now?"

"Fishponds, muh."

Cristol turned and looked at her, her eyes wide. Her tongue licked her bottom lip, her eyes rolled up into her skull, and then rolled back. "D'you should ave stayed away gurl," she said with a dry expressionless voice. "Ne'er looked back. I don't want d'you's ere. When d'you's was taken I missed d'you. Good an proper. Course I did. But… but… but… That was then. Can't go back. Couldn't come and get d'you's. Wouldn't ave been right. I knew what was wrong. I knew what was goen on. Couldn't stop et tisall. Don't blame I for et. Things whir jus the way them was. Sometimes I prayed for d'you's. I don't know if thur be a God. Don't know that at all, but sometimes I reckons thur is, so I prayed. Prayed that et would work out for d'you's. Not for I like, jus d'you's. That d'you'd grow up good and right. Far away from this place. Far away from I, cos I was the problem. I was wrong, cos I can't elp urself. Thur taint no elp for I. I'z ez lost. But d'you's taint. Thur be ope for d'you's. Or thur was. Don't know about now. Anyways I ad no ideawl whir d'you was. Thems didn't tell I nutten. That's the way et was. So couldn't do nutten bout et. Couldn't find d'you's. Didn't know how to look. But I didn't want d'you's comen back, not to this place. D'you's better an that. Better gurl. Better. Kept a photawl of d'you's. Kept et for a long time. But I lost et now. So that's ow et ez. So don't come back. I'm no good for d'you's. Not at all. Member ow weez used to sit on that sofa together, I curled up like a cat in yur lap and d'you's stroking ur hair. I missed that. D'you was good for I then. D'you used to say, 'Don't worry none muh, et'll work out fine.' D'you used to say et. When d'you's was litul. Don't matter none now. Christ, whir the fuck ez Dean?"

All the time that Cristol spoke she didn't look up, her voice fading in and out, the rhythm of her speech slow and slurred. Every now and then she stopped to scratch the back of her hands.

The front door opened and slammed shut. There was the heavy sound of footsteps. Daizee turned to see two men standing in the doorway behind her. They were both unshaven, and shorter than her. One had unkempt hair framing his bald scalp. The other had tired grey hair that could have been painted on with a wire brush. The balder of the two men sniffed.

Cristol shoved passed Daizee and pressed her finger into the bald man's chest. "Whir the fuck d'you's been, Dean? D'you's been fucken ours."

"I got caught up, d'you knows ow et ez," he grinned, "Oo's this?"

"Daizee," snapped Cristol like she'd trapped her in that kitchen especially for them.

"Who?"

"Ne'er mind, what fucken took d'you so long?"

"Alright, keep yur fucken air on."

"I'm fucken dyen ere, Dean."

"I ad to make a deawl, alright, et took fucken time."

The man with the painted on hair was staring at Daizee, dogging her with cold deflated bags for eyes.

"It I up, Noel," begged Cristol to the fella dogging Daizee. "Sort I out an then I'll sort d'you's out."

Noel ignored her, he just kept his stare intently on Daizee.

Daizee didn't like it, not one bit. She looked straight back at him and exaggerated a smile.

Noel turned to Cristol. "Not d'you's," he said. "Err." A dirty grin streaked across on his face.

Cristol looked to Daizee, then to Noel, then back to Daizee. Daizee stared at Cristol from behind her dark glasses. "I don't wanna, muh," she said quietly.

"D'you's didn't tell I d'you's ad a kid. An fuck I what a looker."

"But Noel I'z ez wet," croaked Cristol and stuck her tongue out of her toothless mouth.

"I don't want yur gummy chops on ur cock," spat Noel.

"Et worked alright for d'you's last week."

"Fuck off."

Cristol's face twitched. She sniffed, her hand went first to her nose and then to her hair. Her jaw quivered, her lips moved. She looked at Daizee. Daizee knew exactly what she was going to say before she said it.

"I needs this bad gurl," pleaded Cristol.

"No muh."

"I'm dyen, look a I. D'you knowz what appens to I if I don't get ur it."

Daizee's heart tried to creep back into her doll. But her doll was long gone.

Dean was staring at Daizee too, his face turned into a hungry snarl. "D'you's can do et for yur old muh," he growled. "For ole timez sake."

"Et's just a suck Daizee," begged Cristol, "that's all ee wants."

"Oh muh."

Cristol's tone changed. "If d'you loves I, d'you'll do this for I."

Dean disappeared from Daizee's view for a moment, when he returned he held a machete. "D'you do as yur fucken muh says."

Daizee took in the length of the machete blade, then Dean's pin-high eyes, then her toothless mum. Noel's was standing in the doorway blocking off her escape from the kitchen, with shrivelled hefty limbs and squalid grey hair. He took out a long and brutal looking knife and looked at her with cold eyes.

She knew the lay of the land, knew how to make it easier on herself. There was no point in fighting crazed druggies with a machete and a killer blade. She stood tall, looked Noel in the eye and said, "D'you better wash that cock fore I touches et."

She gobbed it to the floor on her way out of Cristol's squalid bedroom. All she wanted to do was wash her mouth out.

In the bathroom she nearly stumbled into the hole made by a missing floorboard.

In the wreck of that lounge Cristol and Dean had already injected themselves and were collapsed on the sofa. Cristol's skirt was hitched up, the needle sticking out of her groin. Noel emerged out of the bedroom tightening his trouser belt round his consumptive waist. He looked down on Cristol, and Dean, and grinned. He pulled a pipe out of his pocket. "D'you's wants to smoke a rock wiv I?"

Daizee shook her head, she had never liked crack, the way it made people crawl in desperation when it ran out.

"I won't charge d'you for et," he added grinning. "Come on. Do a fucken rock wiv I." He sat himself in the middle of Dean and Cristol.

Cristol opened her eyes then shut them again. Noel built his pipe up, put a nugget of crack into the gauze, put the pipe to his mouth, lit it with a red disposable lighter, pulled on it hard several times, took the smoke deep into his lungs, held his breath and handed the pipe up to Daizee. Daizee shook her head. Noel's eyes bulged, his face strained. He exhaled heavily. "Ave a fucken it," he barked.

Daizee stared at him like she wanted to kill him, grabbed the pipe and took a lungful of the white smoke that smelled like battlefield killer gas. Immediately, it seemed to her, the colours in the room became sharper. There was a tingling in her arms and legs. A cold hand pressed itself against the base of her skull and there was a glowing feeling in her chest and when she breathed the glow became a flame.

Noel showed his corrupted teeth as he pulled a leather pouch out of his pocket and handed it up. "Cook I a little summut," he ordered. He grabbed the pipe back, put his lips to it, lit it, drew a deep breath like it might be his last, then strained his face like he was traversing dimensions at a phenomenal speed.

Daizee knelt on the floor, opened the pouch. It contained a

handful of wraps, a clear bag of rocks and another bag of what looked to her like coke.

Noel stood suddenly and began punching the air.

She took the spoon at Cristol's feet, poured a puddle in it from the bottle that lay beside it. From the pouch she took a wrap, opened it, saw that it was brown, emptied it into the spoon. She paused, looked up.

Noel was in a light fantastic world of his own.

She took another wrap and saw that it too was brown and added that into the potion too. With a lighter, that she took from her own pocket, she boiled the mixture and let it bubble and broil. She pulled the syringe from Cristol's crotch, dipped the needle in, pulled the plunger out and drew in the thick cloudy mix into the shaft. All of it, every single drop.

"Come on then ur sweetz," she said temptingly, toying with the syringe in Noel's face and stroking the inside of his thigh.

Noel dropped his trousers and pants, landed heavily on the sofa, heaved his bollocks aside, and grunted, "Finds yurself a ole," then reached out roughly and pulled her towards himself. She pushed him back, searched his groin for a vein. Found herself a spot. Jabbed the needle in. Noel winced. She pushed the plunger a fraction, then drew out a tiny cloud of thick red blood and heroine, before pushing the concoction home. Noel stuck his tongue out like a demon, his eyes rolled up, his head dropped back and his breath became long and heavy, then quick and sharp. Then coughing. Then a snore. Then silence.

Daizee waited and watched. She stroked the inside of his thigh, fondled him gruffly between his legs. Nothing.

Quickly she frisked his leather jacket, found a screwed up ball of ten and five pound notes, picked up his pouch of drugs and tipped out a wrap of brown – so that Cristol and Dean would have little something to fight over when they came to.

The Romeo & Juliet Killers

She left the flat without shutting the front door.
　She was neither happy nor sad.

2

Knock, knock.

Knock, knock.

"Francis," called his mum.

He was on his bed fully clothed, lying on his stomach, his face tight with dry tears and sleep.

"Francis," called his mum again, "It's me. It's mum. I've some supper for you. Open the door. Please."

He rolled over onto his back and put his arm over his eyes not wanting to get up. Once more she called out. He pulled his knees towards his chest before swinging them over the edge of the single bed. Sitting hunched forward he ran a hand through his hair. He stood reluctantly, crossed the room and flicked the light switch. Then he remembered the icon that he had turned to the wall, which his mum was bound to notice, and turned it back so that it was looking in on the room. Finally he took his chair from under his doorknob, put it under his desk and opened the door. His mum was standing there holding a sandwich on a plate in one hand and a mug of tea in the other.

"It's a cheese sandwich," she said as brightly as she could.

He nodded and sat back down on his bed.

She put the plate and mug down on his desk and turned sheepishly around. "Do you mind if I sit down?"

He shook his head, tucked his feet under himself to give her some room on the end of the bed.

She sat down, looked at him once, half smiled, then stared

ahead of herself, her gaze caught by something on the floor in the corner of the room. Finally she said, "I'm worried about you Francis."

"Mum –"

"No, please, let me finish. I went to see Father Benedict today... He said that your body must be changing, that it must be confusing for you. All these things suddenly distracting you. It must be disorientating. The temptations of the flesh... He said that when it comes on, in a boy, it is quite a shock to the system. You wake up and you have all these urges and you don't know what to do with them or, indeed, how to fight them."

Looking at her hands she went on. "There are some things I must tell you. Things about how we relate to other people. And by we," she added after a nervous pause, "I mean men and women."

Her voice trailed off. Franky could see that she was shaking. Her lips moved as if she was rehearsing a monologue. The voice that finally spoke was weak, unsure and almost inaudible. "When a man joins a woman..."

Franky looked at the wall opposite, at the icon of the Madonna with her teenage baby.

"...The man touches the woman..."

"Yes, mum."

"...A man touches a woman and they join..."

There was a long silence. Finally Franky asked, "Join what, mum? Hands?"

"Yes, yes, they join hands, certainly."

He nodded.

"But it is more than that," she added quickly.

"Right."

"And it can only be undertaken if there is love."

"What can?"
"This intertwining of a man and a woman."
"Intertwining?"
"Yes, Francis. He, the man, touches her, the woman, and his seed fertilises her egg. The seed is very important and should never be wasted."
"Right."
"It is a sin to waste it. And that place of man is not a toy, Francis."
"What place?"
"The place where the seed is housed."
"Like the soul."
"It is like the soul, yes."
Not once had she looked at him.
"I'm not to play with it," he said.
"It is a very serious thing. You do not play with it."
"And where is this toy?"
"In a private place, Francis."
"Ok. I understand."
She didn't say anything more and he was unsure whether she was waiting for any input from him, so he asked, "And then what happens?"
"The baby is born through a hole in the woman."
"What hole?"
"It's a small hole."
"Where?"
She breathed for a moment. Her face scrunched up, she closed her eyes.
Once more he asked, "Where?"
"It's private," she said sharply and rose quickly to her feet. "Right. Ok. I'll leave you to your supper." Pausing at the door she looked back at him and said, "I do love you, Francis, you

do know that, don't you?"

Franky was not entirely sure how he should respond. The conversation had left him disorientated. It seemed to him that he knew more about what she had been talking about than she did.

"Right," she said sadly, turned slowly and shuffled out like a despondent guardian angel.

3

The sunlight was fizzled out and the street lights all puffed up, like late night junky's eyes, as Daizee stepped down from the bus with a headache so thick she didn't want to move. Perhaps it was the rattly old bus, perhaps it was that Noel's crack had worn off. Her black eye was thumping too. Pouring into the quayside were gangs of lads and girls, couples and loners, teens in short leopard-skin dresses and boys with cropped hair in checkered shirts.

She nipped into an all-night shop just up from the Hippodrome, bumped into a gaggle of girls wearing pink horns, porn-star heels and hens-love-cocks on their t-shirts. One of them was holding a half-drunk bottle of Bacardi, stumbling and tottering, much to the cackling amusement of her chums. They all wanted cigarettes, each and everyone of one of them, one by one, laughing and howling. And the laughing got under Daizee's eyes. She pulled a bottle of water from the fridge and, when finally it was her turn, she bought herself a packet of fast-acting Nurofen, the red gel ones with the syrup in, and paid for it with one of Noel's ten pound notes. Out on the street she ripped out four of the soft-centred pills and swallowed them down with the water and winced. They never acted quickly enough. Really she should have just have got a cab back to her bedsit but she couldn't face the smell of cheap air freshener, the quick turns and sudden bumps, so she wandered back down towards the quay and into the first bar she could find, headed straight for the toilets and snorted a couple of mounds of Noel's cocaine off a coin. She started tingling almost immediately but didn't feel any better about the world. Or herself. Her headache still thumping she went to the bar and ordered herself a double vodka and orange. The barman looked strangely at her. She showed him her fake i.d. He glanced at it, then pour her a drink. She knocked it back, ordered another and took herself a seat by the window.

Her legs felt numb. The lights faded, the world about her looked shaded, like an ominous cloud had descended. She was breathless. On the other side of the dock, moored up, a blue-grey war-boat of some kind, she didn't know what, didn't care none either, but focused on it none-the-less, trying to pick out features, the big guns, the stowed lifeboats.

The music was too loud for the emptiness of the bar, pounding drums and some girl wailing on about, "Not getting enough."

"Enough of what," Daizee thought, "I can tell d'you's a fing or two about not getting enuff."

She should have been used to it by then, being let down by her mum, but she wasn't. Seeing Cristol had re-opened a wound. She should have stayed away but she wanted a mum.

She drank her vodka quickly and went back to the toilets, locked herself into a cubicle, put a mound in each nose, shivered, sniffed. She put the toilet seat down, sat and took out Noel's pouch from her coat pocket. There were several small bags of rocks, six wraps of heroin and four wraps of coke. She would keep the coke. She could sell on the wraps of heroin and the bags of crack, not being a fan of either, but instead decided to flush it away because that would be what would piss Cristol off the most. As she emptied each of the wraps into the bowl she imagined Cristol's face, the contortions it would make if she was there to see what she was doing.

Once, when she was little, Cristol opened a wrap too quickly and the brown powder went everywhere and Cristol started screaming and swearing, she was already slimy with sweat and fever, her dealer being late like he always was, and she scrambled about on her hands and knees, in and out of the rubbish that had been thrown there like some third-world-trash mountain, complete with a sewer running straight down the middle of it, and her hands were shaking and Daizee just watched her. How old was she then? Little that's all she could recall, just a little girl with her mutilated doll in her hand watching her mum scrabbling about like her life depended on it, screaming at her not to move, as she scrutinised the floorboards, took up any and every kind of brown powder or fungus and cooked it up and shot it. Her head fell back with a crack, the needle still stuck in her arm, as it always was when she had done too much and Daizee thought for a second that she might be dead, her breathing looked like it had stopped, her chest ceased to rise and fall, her eyes were opened and glazed and kind of peaceful. Then Cristol reached up and snatched her hand, looked into her eyes like she was caught up in a terrifying nightmare, "Who the fuck are d'you's," she said. "Who the fuck are d'you's?"

4

When he was certain that his dad had gone to work, and was not coming back, he cautiously opened the door to his bedroom. Outside in the corridor it was deathly quiet, like the aftermath of some cataclysm. He edged out of his room and sneaked along the dusty carpet, creeping through the valley of piled religious magazines, to the dining room. The door was open. His mum sitting at the dining table, face in hands. He was not sure whether she was praying or crying. An icon audience of gold-encrusted saints watched from the walls.

When he was young he sort of had faith, and the stories his mum told him meant something more than the simple tales of non-existent devils and demons. The trials and torments of the saints were heroic and an example worth following.

And his mum would tell him wondrous tales of impossible deeds, except all of it was possible because Christ rose from the dead, so, if he can do that, of course cripples can walk and water turn to wine.

Seeing his mum sitting there alone, quiet and hunched over brought it all back; how she tucked him into bed at night and told him the story of Samson, with his great mane of spiritual hair, hanging to his waist, and his super-human God-given strength. Back then he had loved that story, though he didn't want to hear too much about Delilah, just the slaughter of armies with the jawbone of an ass.

Where was his dad back then? All he can remember is

his mum taking him shopping, telling him that, no, he can't have that sweet, or crying over his trousers that were torn at the knees because he liked to play football at playtime. They couldn't afford him doing that. Every day she shouted at him before going up to the school to get them to stop him. Which they did, keeping him in at break and lunchtimes until he could prove that he understood.

And then there were days when he caught her crying alone, sitting where she is now.

She looked up, wiped her eyes. "Francis, how long have you been standing there?"

He shrugged his shoulders. "I don't know. Not long."

"Come and sit down."

"What happened, mum?"

"Nothing Francis, he's just worried about you. Sit down. I need to talk to you."

He sat down opposite her. "What did he say to you, mum?"

"It doesn't matter."

"Yes, mum, it does."

"Let me explain Francis."

He braced himself expecting another ticking off.

"God leaves a message within a person, Francis, messages that are only revealed at the moment they are required – that is not to say that God is determining the future – no, that's not it, for it is still up to the person to heed the voice of God, or to discard it. It's more of a clue as to the best possible outcome for your life, rather than an edict from above."

He watched her intently.

"You might think," she went on, "that I met your dad in a church or at some church event, but that is not how it happened."

Franky nodded, she had told him how she met his dad many times and each time he pretended that he was hearing it for the first time.

"I met him at a party in a flat. I don't know how I came to be there, I don't even know who I was with – ah you didn't think that your mum could dance, did you, Francis? In my time... I remember first seeing your dad, he was talking to a friend, smoking a cigarette – yes, he did do that, once. He had thick black hair, which hung down over his ears."

She closed her eyes as if she was picturing Franky's dad as he was then.

"You know for a long time," she continued, "I turned my back on Christ. My years of darkness. Nearly all of my twenties spent in darkness. I stopped going to church, would publicly deny God's existence and then I met your dad and it was as if a little drawer was opened and out popped a tiny envelope. I understood what Magdalene saw when first she looked on Christ. A dazzling purity, the stars, the sun, the canopy of the universe all rolled into one. That is love Francis, not this thing that you were watching."

"Mum –"

"No, listen to me Francis. There is something special about you. You are my gift from God."

He nodded.

"Do you remember that Sunday?"

"What Sunday, mum?"

"Your dad was away and we were praying here. I think you were ill and we couldn't go to church. At one point you stopped me and asked, do you smell that smell? And I said, what smell? And you said, its like roses, but its not roses. As you said that, I smelt it too. And you were right, it was like roses, but it was not roses. It was a profound smell, because it wasn't just a smell, it was the feeling of the smell, and that feeling was like peace. When I looked into your face you were radiant, as if something had touch you, an angel or a saint – No, no, that's not it, that's not it at all. It was like you were in two places at the same time. The other place was heaven and the aroma of heaven was all around you. Other than pointing out the smell to me, you were silent. Silent and attentive, I'm sure you saw something, I could see it in your expression. And then you came round, your eyes focused on me and you smiled. I didn't ask you what had happened, what it was that you had seen. It didn't seem right to ask. I did ask you about the smell of the roses but you had no recollection of them. But that smell had been there, Francis. It had been there. I know it."

Franky shook his head. "I don't remember that."

"That is why you are special, Francis. You have been chosen for something, I don't know what. I suspect it will involve great suffering though. And you will suffer for your faith.

Act III

1

She was smoking a cigarette in front of the Edwardian city museum when she saw him approaching in his school uniform, his heavy school bag slung over his shoulder. Her cigarette dropped to the floor and she stubbed it out with her foot.

The first thing he said was, "What happened to your eye?"

She ignored him, put her arm through his and said, "Why the fuck d'you brings I ere?"

"What's wrong?"

"I don't likes et."

"Why?"

"I jus don't. Taint ur sort a place."

"Why not?"

"Jus taint."

"I come here all the time," he says. "I love it."

"Et's fucken dead."

Behind the green glass of her eyes he sensed a deep anxiety.

"Come with me," he said. "I want to show you something."

"What?"

"Something that puts the fear of God in me."

"What ez et?"

"You'll see."

"I needs a piss first," she said.

"Ok. There's toilets inside."

Entering through the sombre doors stiletto footsteps echoed around the gothic hall and rubber soles squeaked on the old white marble floor.

Daizee disappeared into the Ladies. When she came back out she was sniffing.

Franky led her across the hall, through a narrow corridor passed a dark tomb of a room in which lay the bones of a man that was once a hunter, his bones caked in black tar scabs and the remnants of rotten rags. As they crossed a second hall, from the ceiling of which was suspended a full-size replica of the Wright Flyer lurching towards a crash, Franky said, "It makes me shiver, just walking this way." Daizee failed to answer. When they turned the corner, at the top of the grand marble staircase, Franky's eyes were closed.

"Ha ha ha."

"What's funny?"

"Ets the skeleton of a deer."

"It's a giant deer."

"Et fucken ate grass, Franky."

"It used to give me nightmares."

"Ha ha ha."

"I still don't like coming in here."

"Ha ha ha."

"Stop it."

"Fuck off."

"No you, fuck off," he snapped.

"Don't tell I to fuck off, d'you cuntin about scared of a dead fucken deer." She turned and abandoned him.

He caught up with her outside. She was halfway down Park Street, oblivious to the clothes shops and cafes, heading towards the old docks and the centre of the city. "Daizee, please. I'm sorry."

Her face was tight and there was a burning in her eyes. Her jaw trembled. She dropped her gaze from him to the ground.

"Don't worry bout et," she said quietly, "taint d'you."

"What is it then?"

She pulled a pack of cigarettes out of her pocket, took one out, lit it, blew the smoke out quickly, took another deep drag and blew that out. She rubbed her forehead, bit her bottom lip. "I've bin thur before," she said, her eyes flicked up to him then back to the floor, her shoulders raised and dropped. "With Cristol."

"Who's Cristol?" he asked.

"Ur muh. Err took I. I was a litlun, like four maybe, summut like that. Err was with some fella, I don't know oo. She was beautiful back then. Err seen lots of men. Ee whir tenden et whir a family day out. Thems did fuck off somewhirz. I don't know whir. A fucken room. Oo fucken knows. Thems left I looken at some dead cunt. All that whir left of him whir fucken bones and black pox. And then thur whir shouten and screamen. Et whir ur muh, Cristol, screamen errself a hole in the lung. Thems whir throwen her out. Oo knows what err'd been up to. Two-zen it up, I shouldn't wonder. And I wet urself cos I whir thur on ur tod, with em bones, standen in a pool of ur own piss. That's what appened thur."

She looked at the floor and took quick drags of her cigarette. Her head was bowed and her jaw was tight. Her eyes were moving up and down, to the pavement, to Franky, to the feet of walking shoppers that surrounded them. She was smoking fast. Her eyes strained and red.

"Come on," he said, took her hand and led her into a crowded café, found them a seat in a back corner, at a small wooden table that had once been a sewing machine. Then he went to the counter and bought her a coke. He had to squeeze himself into his seat which was against the wall and watched her as she looked at her glass for a while, circling the edge of it with her finger.

"Are you feeling better?" he asked.

Staring ahead at his chest she shrugged her shoulders, then hunched over her elbows, then she sat back, then turned her face to him. "Why d'you scared of the skeleton of a deer?" she asked.

He thought for a moment. "I don't know," he said. "I just am. I don't like it's face. It freaks me out. I saw it when I was a kid and it terrified me."

"D'yous on yur tod?"

"No. I was with mum. I ran off. Ahead. Turned a corner and there it was. When mum caught up with me I was standing there frozen to the spot."

"What err do? Laff?"

"Mum? No. She picked me up and gave me a kiss." He looked at the counter and the queue of people, the bank of cakes and sandwiches. "Funny," he said, "I'd forgotten all about that."

"What?"

"That mum was there."

"Et must be nice," she said, "to ave yur muh do that."

"Do what?"

"Not leave d'you standen in yur own piss."

"She wouldn't do that," he said. Suddenly aware that the café's crowded he lowered his voice and added, "It's not all good."

She nodded but her eyes flicked away.

"They're mad. My parents."

"So?"

"Everyone else's parents are normal but mine are weird."

"What's weird about em?"

He shuffled in his seat.

"Yur blushen," she said smiling.

"Am I?"

"Yeh," she chuckled, "tell I."

He looked down at the table. "They're religious."

"What like happy clappy?"

"No. They're Catholic."

"Right," she said, not really understanding him.

He breathed out.

"D'you might need to get over et," she said.

"What?"

"Yur folks. Them's thur. Even if ets a little fucked up, taint nasty fucked up."

"You'd understand if d'you met them," he said.

"I won't be meeten em," she half laughed.

"Why not?"

"I jus won't," she said turning away.

2

He had no idea what the film was about. His attention was captivated by Daizee who was sitting beside him, twisting her short hair with her finger and spooning popcorn into her mouth, engrossed. She hardly noticed him, at least that's what he thought. Every time she laughed it brought a smile to his face.

"What d'you's looken at?" she said suddenly like an apparition popping up to say boo.

Franky was certain that he had lit up bright enough to ruin the film for all six of the other audience members.

"What?" she said again.

"Nothing."

"D'you's been watchen I right through the flick."

"Have I?"

"D'you knows et."

"Do you mind," said a voice behind them.

"Mind what?" Daizee snapped.

"This is a cinema."

"Fuck I Einstein, I thought et whir a fucken beach." She winked at Franky.

"What did you say?" said the voice.

"D'you's right, I'm fucken with d'you's. Ur sweetheart ere whir gonna to tell I that ee luvs I, whirnt d'you Franky?"

"What?" Franky shrank into his seat.

"Well don't d'you's?"

"Don't I what?"

"Luvs I."

"Please, I really am trying to watch the film," hissed the voice behind.

"An ee really ez trying to tell I that ee luvs I, taint d'you's?" Franky was looking at her stumbling over his thoughts.

"Come on Franky," she said, "say et."

"Yes.'

"Yes what?"

"I love you."

She looked to the seat behind them. "See. All done." She turned back to the film, shoved her hand into the popcorn, took a handful, stuffed it into her mouth.

Franky sat back. "So this is what love feels like," he thought. He'd made it. Always he had feared that he would never find love with a girl, assuming that it was well beyond his reach, that he would never discover the right person, or that he was not man enough, not like the boys at school who carried their conquests around on their mobile phones. In the dark of the cinema with the colours of the moving images flickering on his face he imagined that anything was possible.

Something flicked against his face. He was back in the cinema. It flicked again. Turning to face her a piece of popcorn flicked off his cheek. There was a big broad grin on her face. Dumbstruck he smiled back at her. It was then that she kissed him on the cheek with a quick peck, followed up with a kiss on his lips, followed by a wink before she reached out and popped a piece of popcorn into his open mouth.

3

"That's Spain," said Franky pointing to where Daizee was looking, his school tie hung about his neck like a dancer in repose.

They were standing at the top of Cabot Tower. Directly below them Brandon Hill dropped away towards the refurbished quayside and just the other side of the docks, like a giant ship-in-a-bottle stood Isambard Kingdom Brunel's magnificent steamship, the SS Great Britain.

"Eh?" she said looking confused.

"Look," he said running his hand over a brass plate with arrows and place names engraved into it. Pointing to the left of some housing estate in the distance he added, "And over there is Australia."

"Whirz et say that?"

"It doesn't, but if that's where Madrid is, then Australia's just a few miles on that way."

"Bet et's more an few miles."

"Alright, then, it's the other side of the world."

"How long d'you reckons et takes to get thur then, eh Mistur Shakespeares?"

"I don't know."

"Come on, d'you knows everthing, Franky."

"Twenty four hours, on a plane, all day and all night."

"For real?"

"Yeah."

"Fuck."

"Yeah."

"I'm gonna get thur," she said.

"Yeah?"

"Yeh, totlee. Get the fuck out of this place."

"They're making a plane," he said, "that will do it in two hours. It'll fly up, outside the atmosphere and just wait for the earth to turn. And then it will come back down."

"Magic," she said.

"Daizee Byatt d'you fucken whore betch," cracked a voice from behind them.

Franky saw the light fall out of Daizee's face. He turned to see a man with scrawled on grey hair and a face like a trampled glove. In his right hand he held an enormous knife.

"Put ya fucken shank away d'ya cunt," she snapped.

"Oo the fuck is ee?" snarled Noel, bearing his teeth and pointing the sharp tip of his knife at Franky.

"Fuck off, Noel," she said.

Franky stepped between them both. "Who are you?" he said trying his hardest not to shake.

"Oo am I? Oo am I? I'm Noel fucken West d'you fucken little cunt," and he poked the blade under Franky's chin.

"Leave im the fuck alone," she screamed.

"D'you fucken up im now?" spat Noel and he flicked his tongue in the air like a snake's, almost licking Franky's nose.

Franky stumbled back. "Daizee?" he cried.

He felt a hand on his shoulder push him forcibly out of the way. Turning he saw the green pool of Daizee's eyes had become cool and inviting, but they weren't inviting for him, she was looking directly at Noel. She coyly bit her bottom lip. "Doesum wants to touch I, Noel?" She coo'd calmly before gently hissing her breath in, like she was sucking pleasure out of the air. "Ez that what d'you's wants?"

"I'm gonna do more an that," he seethed, "whirz ur fucken gear?"

"I don't knows nuttens about that?" teased Daizee, as she calmly took her coat off, held it out then let it drop to the floor.

"What the fucks d'you doen?" hissed Noel.

"What the fuck d'you's finks?"

Noel's look darted to Franky. The look made Franky flinch.

"Don't worry none, ur sweetz," said Daizee to Noel in a caramel voice, "thurs only one fing this cunts wants," she pointed her nose at Franky. "Ee wants to watch us. Fucken filthy, taint ee? Doesum wants im to watch us? Ee likes to watch, don't d'you's, ur luver?" She moaned and casted an eye to Franky. "D'you's can fucks I Noel an ee can watch. Gurt lush or what?"

She slowly began to take her t-shirt off. Franky wanted to rush forward to stop her but he had no movement in his body. She lifted her t-shirt over her head, to reveal a red bra. She held the t-shirt out and dropped it at Noel's feet. A slight breeze blew through her hair as she put her hand on her left breast and began to massage it, pinching the nipple. The expression on her face shuddered.

"Doesum wants us to take yur troozers off?" she purred. "Doesum likes that?"

Noel's face broke into a filthy grin.

"Doesum wants to put that shank on ur skin?"

Noel's jaw tremored.

"Good, I wants d'you to."

She unbuttoned her jeans, slid them off to reveal her black thong with a little red bow at the front.

It shocked Franky at how comfortable she was with next to nothing on. "Daizee," he said, "what are you doing?"

"Shut up," she snapped at him, her eyes looking all intent and fierce. She looked at Noel and those eyes melted into oozing pools of pleasure. "Doesum likes the way I spokes to im?"

Noel's eyes looked to Franky and then back to her.

She ran a finger slowly from her chest to the front edge of her thong and toyed with the small bow.

Noel's tongue was on his lips.

"What a puppy dawg look," she drawled as she made to lower her thong with her thumbs, gently moving her buttocks to music that only Noel could hear.

The knife quivered and then it was gone. Daizee just reached forward and took it. "D'you silly cunt," she squawked.

Noel made one swipe with his fist, Daizee ducked, Franky charged forward with his eyes closed like a little boy in his first scrap, wrapped his arms around Noel's torso and lifted him with every bit of strength he possessed, heaving him over the parapet barrier. Noel was screaming like a soul just damned to hell. Franky opened his eyes to find that Noel had grabbed the wrought iron frame with one hand, his other gripping his back, trying to drag him over the edge with him and Franky was punching and punching but Noel wouldn't let go, so Franky bit into the hand on the bar. The pitch of Noel's screams changed. Franky felt the grip on his back loosen, he bit harder, tasted blood and pushed with everything he had. And Noel fell, howling, arms flaying, his legs running. He flipped on the first floor balcony below which somersaulted him into a broken bag of bones and spilt brains, his arms twisted, his legs in a dreadful dead man's twitch.

Daizee dropped Noel's knife, pulled Franky away from the parapet. "Cummon," she said. She was already halfway through putting her jeans back on. Buttons up, reaching for her t-shirt.

Franky's hands were shaking, his legs all wobbly. "What have I done?" he gasped.

"Nutten," she spat quickly and grabbed him by the hand, pulled him through the door, and down the stone staircase. He yanked her still.

"What the fuck d'you's doen?" She shouted.

"I need to think."

"Don't worry bout im."

He closed his eyes. He could still feel Noel's hands grappling with his body.

"Franky, cummon."

His voice faltered. "But you... you – I didn't know what's what – I didn't know you."

"Et whir an act, Franky, an now ee's a deader, so fuck im."

"Who was he?"

"Et don't matter none."

"I'm not going anywhere til you tell me who he was."

"Shit, Franky, get a fucken grip."

"Tell me."

She looked away, closed her eyes, then looked back hard and serious, "I scuttles urself, Franky, alright," and her hands made a useless desperate gesture like what she'd just said would change everything between them. There were tears in her eyes too. The look on her face turned cold. She grabbed him by the chest, pulled him down the spiral staircase, put her arm around him and pushed him out of the darkness of the tower into the cold light of day.

4

I want to go home," he said as they ran through a leafy square, just outside the tower park.

"D'you what?"

"I want to go home. My parents will know what to do."

"Nah."

"They'll help us."

"Ow's them gonna elp, Franky?"

"They'll look after us."

"Oh fuck off."

Yanking his hand free of hers he stopped. By his side there was a wooden bench. Behind that the scarred stump of a felled tree, a green metal fence with spears for fence posts. They were overlooked by windows with shut white blinds, lines of slits that fingers could easily part. In the distance came the sound of sirens getting closer. He sat abruptly on the bench.

Looking down on him she took her pack of cigarettes out of her coat pocket, looked nervously to the left and right of her. "Weez can't stay ere, Franky."

He ignored her. "Do you think he felt anything?"

"Nah."

"How do you know?"

"I don't give a fuck."

"Not even a little bit. He's dead."

"Keep yur voice down."

He stood, took a couple steps forward, put his hands

through his hair, pulled his scalp tight then put his hands out in front of him, stretched them out and stared at them. "We can't go home now. It's too early. I should be in school. If we went home now, they would know that something was wrong. Are you sure he's dead?"

"Cummon, Franky."

"He might be sitting there, right now, alive."

"Franky, ee landed on iz fucken ed."

"People have been known to survive falls like that."

"Stop et Franky, d'you's freaken I out."

"Was he really that bad?"

"Not a good bone en ez body."

He put his forehead in his hands again and stared wildly at the ground. "They might just think he killed himself."

"D'you reckon?"

"Why not?"

"D'you's did a good job of tryen to bite the fucker's and off, for one fing. Cummon, weez gotta go."

Completely out of the blue he said, "You were different."

Her eyes blinked, her brow strained impatiently. "When?"

He paused like he was afraid to say whatever it was he had to say, and that pause made her scared of whatever it was he was thinking. "When you'd taken your clothes off."

Her eyes narrowed as she looked at him. "D'you like et?"

"Why would I like it?"

"Most fellas do."

"Is that what you think of me?"

"Nah, sweetz," she whispered, "d'you's taint like no one I'z ever met before."

"You called him that."

"What?"

"Sweets."

"Didum?"
"You know you did."
"So? I call everone that, et don't mean nutten."
"Doesn't it?"
"What's up?"
He looked away from her. "It's nothing."
She pulled his face back round. "Yeh tis."
The sirens had got to where they were going, probably somewhere at the foot of the hill below the tower. Not quite close by, but close enough.

What he said next surprised her. "I'm sorry. I didn't do anything. If I had done something, then maybe, you wouldn't have had to take your clothes off for him. I could have stopped that. I could have stopped him from forcing you to do that."

She glanced at a passing couple, then pulled him by the shirt close to herself, forehead to forehead. "Look Franky, thur taint nutten d'you could ave done. Ee ad a knife. I done what I ad to do. Thur whirnt nutten wrong wiv what d'you's did. Fuck most kids would ave been frozen to the spot and pissen thur pants."

"I was."

She took his face in her hands and held it close to hers. "Nah, d'you whirnt. I mean, fuck, for some one that whir scared d'you fought him like a proper ero. D'you come froo. If thats d'you being scared then thurs nutten wrong wiv bein scared, Franky."

"Who was he?"

She let his head go and stepped back. "Franky, weez got to go."

"Who was he?"

She shook her head. "Jus someone."

"He had a knife, Daizee."

She flinched, it was a tiny, almost imperceptible flinch, but he saw it. "I can't talk about et," she said.

"What does that mean?"

"Nutten."

"Come on, Daizee, please."

She looked away, breathed out, looked back at him and nodded. "Ee wanted summut off I, Franky… Summut which I took… Because of summut ee done."

They heard laughter. She quickly grabbed his hand and pulled him in the opposite direction.

Act IV

1

There is a memory that Franky always recalled when he feared that he may have done something horrific, or stupid, or just plain wrong. In it he is standing hand in hand with his mum, in front of the white marble altar of the Catholic Cathedral of Bristol. His mum had said, "The very nature of God is love. That is why his mercy is infinite. Because his love has no end."

"What about evil people?" he had asked.

"Well," his mum answered, "it is certainly harder for people like Hitler. I was thinking more about people who have done little things, or had sin thrust upon them. When considering the sins of people I think you have to retain some feeling for their given circumstances and ask yourself what were the big motivations of their lives, was it just them or was it the people and events surrounding them? Sometimes I think there are mitigating circumstances behind sin and I am sure that God thinks this too. That is why there is purgatory, so that a soul maybe purified before it ascends to heaven."

Entranced by her story he had asked, "What happens in purgatory?"

"Well," said his mum smiling, clearly enjoying the effect that she was having on him, "you sort of get punished there, but its not like the punishment of hell, it is only finite and it is a punishment designed to purify, whereas in hell it is designed to punish and, of course that punishment is eternal, it never ends. Those who pass through purgatory, which will probably be most of us (because none of us are so completely pure that we can simply stroll straight into heaven and hang up our coats), will endure all manner of torments, safe in the knowledge that before long they will bathe directly in the light of God's love and I think," she added, "that a little bit of that light shines down on purgatory to soothe some of the pain away, because God is good and really can't endure the suffering of those he loves." Whenever Franky was in trouble it was this that brought him home.

But when Franky's mum clapped eyes on Daizee it was obvious to Franky, if it hadn't been before, that there was a limit to his mum's sense of altruism and Christian charity. She took one look at Daizee and clearly didn't like what she saw and made no attempt to hide her displeasure.

Daizee stuck out her hand to say, "I'z pleased to meet d'you," and her t-shirt tightened over her breasts. Franky mum's eyes widened and her brow crinkled up in disgust. Obviously Daizee saw this and Franky saw that Daizee saw. He saw too that Daizee shrank, ever so slightly. This was not the Daizee that felt comfortable with herself with next to nothing on, on top of Cabot Tower.

And it seemed to him that his mum enjoyed the effect she was having. Whatever Daizee was about to say or do, it would be entirely wrong and inappropriate, and his mum would revel in her discomfort. His mum had that effect on people. His mum had that effect on him. She ignored Daizee's hand, which made Franky furious. But too much had already happened that day for him to say anything, or raise a protest. He was too confused. Too distraught.

Daizee glanced at Franky then back to his mum, "D'you's got a nice flat. Et's cosy."

"Is it?" replied Franky's mum coldly.

"Yeh."

"And where do you live, Daizee?"

"Oh out Fishponds way."

Franky's mum nodded. "And what do your parents do?"

Daizee shrugged her shoulders. "I don't live with em."

Franky's mum glanced at Franky with this supercilious expression on her face. "Really? Why's that?"

"Oh d'you knows."

"And your eye? What happened to your eye?"

"I bumped into a lamp post."

Franky's mum nodded. It was a nod that Franky had seen before, when someone said something about a subject that appalled and disturbed her, like abortion, or the lack of religious teaching in schools, or the over sexualisation of sex education, or equal rights for homosexuals. Or when he was a boy, if ever they were stopped, as she tried to rush him out, in order for Franky to receive an invitation to tea, or a party, to which he was only allowed to go to once he had received a series of lectures, not on the do's and don'ts of his behaviour, but the moral dissolution he must avoid, because all those mothers were feminist modernisers who sought a greater, deeper, liberalisation of society and the church and, "One or two," she had declared, hushing her voice to a whisper, "even voiced their desire to see women priests within the Catholic fold. How ridiculous," she exclaimed, "a woman in church vestments, just look at those stupid women of the Church Of England – they look like clowns!"

2

When Franky's mum asked Daizee if she prayed, Daizee couldn't help but blink. She had been asked that question before, by a preacher she used to see once in a while.

Each time he saw her he would give her a flower, and each time he would tell her how much more beautiful she was than the last time they met.

He was like any other man until after the sex when, almost at the very moment of climax, he would fall to his knees, if he was not there already, and break out in prayer, forcing Daizee to join him.

Rocking backwards and forwards, he begged the Almighty to save his soul, and then he would start in on her. Not blaming her, just wanting her to forgive him, and then he would preach to her about God and the Devil, and heaven, all of which she was never likely to see, on account of what she did for a living. She didn't really know about God and the Devil, but when it came to heaven, she was certain that it was just like the song, and what you actually needed to get in there was cash, and lots of it. She'd seen it in magazines and once or twice a punter had given her a glimpse of what it was like on the other side, though that didn't feel much like heaven to her, if she was honest about it.

She got used to that man of God and she became quite relaxed around him, even though he would start praying after each and every intimacy. At least, she said to herself, he was predictable. Then one day he did not pay her up front. First rule of business is get your cash before you get down to it. To begin with she didn't think too much of it, because he was a regular and it seemed rude to say, "Pay I first, then fuck I".

He did his business in her, and then, as was his want, he started off on about God, but there was something different about him this time, something out of control. He forced her to kneel as he went on about her soul being like a small bird that had got lost on its journey – "Whir I'z ez goen in the first place," she thought, "ez anybody's guess," but she knelt with him anyway and let him put his hand on her head, then all over her. She thought, "This is a bit weird," especially when he started singing and wailing about her being fallen, but she thought, "what the fuck, customer's always right." It was when she raised the subject of money with him that it all came out.

He didn't have any. Not a penny. And he didn't have a job anymore because his church had fired him. Not only that but his wife had left him and taken the kids with her. He had lost everything.

It was all to do with Daizee. Someone had discovered that he was using church funds to pay for her and at least one other prostitute, though quite how many Daizee never found out.

It was then that he asked her if she believed in God and if she prayed.

And she thought for a moment, considering the question carefully. "Yeah, she said, "sometimes. D'you knows thurs times when d'you jus needs thur to be a God, that wipes away some of the shit in the world. I don't know exactly ow, cos on the surface nutten changes. Fellas still goes about thur wrongs like, but summut inside ez different. Et's a shame cos a bit of prayer can't change nutten, or stop a person oo's set on urten d'you's, or scumming d'you's up like, but summut inside ez different, after et don't seem so bad. Mind d'you, sometimes I kind of wish God would pull iz finger out and jus get rid of em tossers oo's causen proper grief for the rest of us that jus wants to live life quiet like. But then I guess if et was that easy, why ave the promise of eaven. Life's no meal ticket. Ez et?"

It crossed her mind to pass this onto Franky's mum but she thought better of it and instead looked a little lost and looked to Franky to help her out. Which Franky did.

3

"Is it alright if Daizee stays?" he asked.

"What?" said his mum like she was coming round from a knockout blow.

"Daizee needs somewhere to stay tonight, I said it would be alright that she stays here."

His mum blinked. "I'll have to talk to your dad."

Franky turned to Daizee and smiled gently, "Would you like a cup of tea?"

Daizee nodded a weak nod.

His mum said, well spat it really, like she was trying to regain control of the situation, "When you've made your friend a cup of tea, I would like to talk to you, Francis. Alone, please. I'll be with your dad in his study."

And that was it, his mum was off into the gloom of the flat. Franky and Daizee were left standing in the stunned silence of the living room, with all those saints looking on.

"It'll be alright," he said at last, but without any real conviction in his voice.

There was another silence.

This time it was Daizee who spoke first in a hushed whisper, "Weez can't stay ere Franky. Yur muh taint avin none et."

"It'll be fine," he said.

"D'you see the way she looked at I?"

Franky nodded.

"Et taint gonna to work, Franky, et jus taint."

He nodded again. And again there was this long silence. Daizee looked about the room. In the corners were books piled on the floor and magazines gathering dust.

"What's all em about?" she asked, as a way of breaking the ice.

"God. The history of God."

"Ee gets about," she said.

"Yeah, haven't you heard, he's everywhere."

"Not everwhir," she said.

"No?"

"No. Trust I."

"Come on," he said and took her through a door to the small kitchen. Took the stainless steel kettle to the sink, filled it, put the kettle on the stand and flicked it on.

"Et's kind of nice ere," she said. "Yur muh's got a bit of a plank up her cunt, but apart from that et's alright. Wiv all them books. Weird, but nice. Ave em read all them books?"

"Yeah, I think so."

"Fuck, them must knowz a fing or two."

"No, not really. They know a lot about religion and heaven and stuff like that. Mum does read novels and talks about the characters like they're real people. She says the novel explores the rights and wrongs of things so that you can see what would happen to you, if you did what a character did. But the thing is, she only reads old books, stuff that was written like over a hundred years ago, so it don't really mean anything anymore. Things have changed."

The kettle boiled. Once the tea was poured he said, "Right, I'd better take these to them. You'd better wait here."

"Sure fing."

She followed him anyway, silently through the flat. When they arrived at the door to the study they could hear whispering inside. Franky stopped. Stared at the door, bit his top lip. "It might be better if you stay in the kitchen."

"I'll wait ere."

"No. Don't. I know them."

"Go on, I'll be orright. Et won't be nutten I taint ever eard before."

"No?"

"I've seen yur muh's cards, Mr Shakes." And she smiled. "Ok?"

He took a deep breath, smiled and nodded that he was ready. She reached out, turned the door handle for him. The whispering within stopped. He nudged the door open just wide enough for him to walk through before pushing it shut behind him.

4

Through the keyhole Daizee spied Franky standing in front of his parents who were looking cold and severe, his dad's head bald was like a shiny egg, with a thin ring of curls to either side. His mum's short bob was cut to an edge so sharp it could have been a razor.

As he cleared his throat, the expression on Franky's dad's face was that of an affronted puritan. "Where did you go?" he demanded of Franky.

"I needed to get out," said Franky.

"Out? I was not aware that you were allowed out. Is this out during the school day? Or did you wait until it was done."

"I went after school."

"Did I not order you to come home straight from school?"

"Yes – but."

"Yes – but what?"

"Something happened."

"Something happened?"

"Yes."

"I take it this something was this girl that your mum has told me about?"

"Yes."

There was a long silence. Franky's dad observed his son, his eyes narrowed. "And who is she?"

"A friend."

"She looks like a prostitute," hissed his mum.

"Please Deirdre," proclaimed Franky's dad slowly, "I will deal with this."

"She's not a prostitute," said Franky clearly trying not loose his temper.

"Where is she now?"

"In the kitchen."

"Are you sure?" snapped his mum.

"Yes."

"She might be walking around looking for things to steal."

"What have we got that's worth stealing?" said Franky sarcastically.

"Thank God there's no money in the house."

"Deirdre, please," said Franky's dad contemptuously, "I don't want to have to tell you again."

Franky's mum drew in a long breath. Her jaw was clenched tight, her neck was tense.

"Does it surprise you that we're upset?" asked Franky's dad.

Franky shrugged his shoulders.

"Don't shrug your shoulders at me Francis, I asked you a question."

"No, but –"

"Well that's it then."

"You don't understand."

"What don't I understand? That you were caught watching questionable material at school, that you are unruly, and now you are standing here having disobeyed me? You are grounded Francis. That is right isn't it? Not only have you disobeyed me, you went out to galavant with some girl who has clearly disturbed your mum. Who is she?"

"Her name is Daizee."

"I know that, Francis, who is she?" he shouted.

"She's just someone I met."
"Today?"
"No."
"When?"
"Last week."
"When last week?"
"Just last week."
"How old is she?"
"My age."
"And which school does she go to?"
"I don't know."
"What do you mean, you don't know? I would have thought it would be an inevitable conversation opener for children of your age."
"It wasn't."
"Does she go to school? Your mum has told me that she is not wearing a school uniform."
"No, she's not wearing a uniform."
"That would imply that she does not go to school."
Franky held his ground, but said nothing. His dad scowled. His mum shifted on her seat, her cheek was twitching.
"What about her parents?" started Franky's dad again.
"What about them?"
"Why is she here and not with them?"
"She doesn't live with them."
Franky's dad's eyes narrowed. "What do you mean she doesn't live with them?"
"Just that."
"Is she in care?"
"She has been, but not anymore."
"So who does she live with now?"
"She lives alone."

His mum couldn't hold it anymore. "I want that girl out of my house, it took me one look to see that she's trouble. I want her out of my home."

"No," said Franky suddenly. "If you are the Christians you say you are, then you will let her stay."

His dad stiffened, his mum gasped. "I beg your pardon?" they said in unison.

"Good Christians help people. You taught me that's what faith is all about. That it's about love and charity and doing things for other people. Daizee needs somewhere to stay tonight. I invited her. This is my home too."

"You live in our house!" shouted his mum.

"Deirdre, I have told you," screamed his dad, "you are not helping matters. I will deal with this. If you had kept more of an eye on him then we would not be sitting here now. This is your fault."

Franky's mum was on her feet. "I can't put up with this."

Franky's dad exploded, "Then shut up woman." His eyes bulged, his body compressed, his fist came down hard on the arm of his chair. "How many times do I have to tell you? How many times must you interrupt me, I said I will deal will this, so I will deal with this, I don't need to hear what you have to say, I know exactly how you feel, and it is not helping matters, so please keep your mouth shut, you have caused enough trouble already."

"How dare you, Peter, this is nothing to do with me. I have done my very best to bring up our son, and support you, and all I get in return is your contempt. I can't stand it any longer."

"You know where the door is!"

Franky's mum's hand went to her mouth, her shoulders began to shake, tears flooded from her eyes.

Franky looked away at the bookcase that stood against

the wall and waited for her to stop crying. He could not bring himself to look at his dad, he hated the way his dad treated her. When his mum was halfway recovered he said, "You've always said that if a person needs help, then we should help. You told me that that is what the bible teaches us. This is the example that Christ gave us. It doesn't matter who it is, if someone needs help they need help."

His dad looked at him and then asked softly, "Does this girl need help, Francis?"

"Yes," said Franky without a hint of weakness in his voice, "she needs help."

5

Daizee didn't know what to say when the food was placed in front of her by Franky's mum. The grilled cod was burnt around the edges, the potatoes were dry and powdery, and the runner beans looked liked they were made of rubber. She stared at them, then glanced up to Franky. Franky smiled nervously at her. She was aware that his dad was watching her too.

"Et looks nice," she said to Franky's dad. She should have have said it to Franky's mum, but it was clear that no attempt at niceties was going to rescue their relationship, and anyway she didn't care for her feelings.

"What was your name, child?" asked Franky's dad.

"Daizee," said Daizee uncomfortably.

"Daizee? Now that is a nice name. A summer name. When one closes one's eyes, one thinks of cloudless skies and rolling meadows."

Daizee glanced at Franky, caught his eye. He dropped his gaze to his plate.

"I'm sorry if you don't like fish," said Franky's dad.

"I'z orright with fish."

"I'm glad to hear it," replied Franky's dad. "Today is our day of fast."

She nodded not really knowing what he was talking about. She looked to Franky, whose face was white and his cheeks crimson. He didn't know where to look.

"Do you know what a fast is, Daizee?" asked Franky's dad.

"Please Peter," said Franky's mum impatiently, "the food is getting cold."

"Deirdre, I was going to explain something important to Francis's friend." He smiled provocatively at her, then he turned back to Daizee. "Fasting, my dear Daizee, is a good habit to get into."

Franky's mum breathed out angrily.

Franky's dad stood suddenly, followed quickly by Franky's mum. Franky's dad looked to Daizee. "Please would you join us as we give thanks for what we are about to eat."

Daizee looked at Franky who nodded and stood. Daizee stood. Franky's dad held out his hand for her. She hesitated before taking it. Franky's dad threw a steely look to Franky's mum. She held out her hand for Daizee to take. They both then held out their hands to Franky. And they stood there in a circle holding each other's hands as Franky's dad said a few words of thanks, followed by a moment of silence before Franky's parents sat. Franky nodded shyly to Daizee that it was ok for her to sit.

Daizee pushed her food around her plate. Franky's parents ate with their heads down. Daizee looked up at Franky, whose face had drained of colour, when a muffled drumbeat began to sound, augmented by a whispering, before a soft clear male voice began to sing:

> *"Ooh baby, I'm hot like an oven*
> *I need some lovin*
> *And baby, I can't hold it much longer*
> *It's getting stronger and stronger."*

"What's that?" hissed Franky's mum. Franky's dad's eyes were wide open in shock.

The colour had left Daizee's face. She was trying to suppress her laughter.

> *"And when I get that feeling
> I want sexual healing."*

"Et's ur fone," said Daizee only just able to control herself.

"Could you turn it off, please," ordered Franky's mum. "I do not like them. I do not allow my son to possess one and I refuse to have them in the house."

Daizee took her phone out of her pocket and the song became louder and clearer.

> *"Get up, get up, get up, get up
> Let's make love tonight."*

"I do not want that at the table," seethed Franky's mum.

Daizee shut the sound off.

"It might be better, Daizee," said Franky's dad calmly, "if you put it in your coat in the wardrobe in the hall. That way you will not be tempted to get it out, and our peace will not be disrupted."

Daizee glanced at Franky.

"That is, if you want to stay here," added Franky's mum coldly.

Daizee forced a smile at her, went out into the hall, opened the dark wardrobe, found her coat, placed her phone into a pocket before returning to her place.

Franky's dad smiled at her, "We are a little old-fashioned here, Daizee, it is hard enough to escape the outside world as it is, so we like to insist that it is well and truly left outside."

Franky's mum said nothing, she glared at her plate.

Franky's dad glanced at her when he finished speaking before resuming his meal.

There was a long silence through which they ate. Or at least Franky's mum and dad ate. Franky's dad chewed his food carefully. Franky's mum just put the food in her mouth and it seemed that she could not bear to chew it. Franky looked at his mum before looking pleasantly back to Daizee, and tried to reassure her with a smile.

"You can have a pair of Francis's pyjamas," said Franky's mum breaking the silence.

"I don't do jamas," said Daizee without thinking about what she was saying.

"You will wear them," asserted Franky's mum, "if you are to stay here."

Daizee looked Franky's mum in the face. Her jaw clenched. She glanced to Franky who looked like he might fall apart at any minute. And it was for him that she looked back at his mum and nodded that she would do as she was asked.

"Good," said Franky's mum. "When I have finished my supper, I will make up the sofa for you."

6

Daizee lay wide awake and furious. Franky's mum had forced her to undress, and put Franky's pyjamas on, with her in the room. Even though Franky's mum had turned her back on her, it felt to Daizee that she was watching her, looking at her body.

There was a gentle knock on the door.

"It's me," Franky whispered. "You ok?"

"This sofa is fucken mank," she said.

He stood in the doorway without saying anything. She could not see his face though it was obvious to her that there was something wrong.

He crossed the room in the near darkness. "Budge up," he said, and began to crawl onto the sofa with her.

"Whirs yur folks?"

"Bed."

"D'you sure, thems'll will get proper mentalist if em finds d'you's in ere, let alone in ur bed."

"Let them," he said and tucked himself in next to her, "they're the least of our worries." She awkwardly put her arm around him letting his head rest against her chest.

"I think we should go to the police," he said quickly.

"What brought that on?"

"If we go to the police, then we can tell them the truth, that it was self defence. Noel went up there with a knife and was going to kill us."

"D'you finks thems'll believe d'you?"

"Why not?"

She remained silent not knowing what to say to him. Nothing good ever came from having anything to do with the police. "I can't, Franky."

"Why?"

"Because of what I'z ez. Because of whirs I come from. Because of whir I got to go back to when etz all done an dusted, assumen that ez them lets us out, which taint guaranteed, in fact etz most unlikely, considering."

"Considering what?"

"Let it go, Franky."

"How can you be so certain?"

She breathed out. Her heart had begun to beat very fast. There was a quiver to her breath that juddered her first whispered words... "Yur muh got I jus about right when she said I'z looks like a prostitute... I'z ez a prostitute... I does that." She let out a trembling breath... "I does sex for monee... I'm not proud of et, Franky. But I taint ashamed none either. Etz oo's I am. Jus so d'you knows, I dint let no one touch I. Not at first. Thems jus did et whether I liked et or not. That's the fing, innum. Choice. I ad none. Cristol, ur muh dint keep err eye out for I. Dint look to see what was going on. Then things went the way them does and she used I to get what she needed. She ad fellas and that and them would do fings... Would want fings. Et got bad so I got put into care. D'you'd have fort, like, that fings would start to get better, but them dint. All us in care whir all the same. Et's all us knew. And some of the older ones whir making it work, like, and them showed us the ropes and... that was that."

Franky lay back and stared at the ceiling not really sure what to say. "I'm sorry," he said at last.

"Taint d'your fault Franky."

"I know. I've had it quite easy really. My parents are just weird."

"We az what weez az, and weez deals with et."

"What do you mean?"

"That d'your folks taint just weird, Franky, thems fucked right up."

He let out a laugh, "I guess they are. I did warn you."

"No, d'you forgot to mention that when d'you's was desparate to drags I ere."

"You don't mind me bringing you here."

'Nah. Mind d'you, d'your muh tis a bit of work. But she's a saint compared to mine. Anyway, fanks."

"For what?"

"Savin I. Today."

"Did I?"

"D'you totally did Mister Shakespeares."

"I like it when d'you calls me that."

"Does ya, Mr Shakes?"

"Yes, Daizee, I does," he said mimicking her.

7

Daizee was screaming. Franky's mum had pulled her up by her hair like she'd landed a sewer rat.

Still half asleep Franky wasn't sure what was happening. "Mum don't," he shouted.

His mum tore away Daizee's pyjamas, the top first, then the bottoms. Daizee was stripped naked, his dad was in the corner of the room, looking shocked, the bottom half of his pyjama top sliced open, his hairy belly bared.

"What d'you's fucken looken at," screamed Daizee, advancing on Franky's dad, "ad a good fucken look," and she put her hand on her crotch, "d'you's wanna gander up ur cunt?!!"

Franky half expected his dad to start shouting, but he didn't he just stood there looking bemused and out of his depth. Instead it was his mum that was blistered with an anger that she couldn't control. She flung Daizee's clothes at her, yelling, "Get out," then screaming it, "get out!"

Franky cried, "Stop it, stop it." Tears were burning his cheeks, his eyes stung, his body was shaking. He wanted to put his arms around Daizee, but his mum was between him and her.

He picked Daizee's clothes up from off the floor, pushed his mum aside, handed Daizee her clothes, put his hand on her cheek. "I'm sorry," he said softly. He turned to face his mum. "Get out," he said, "get out and let her dress."

"I'm not leaving you in here with that," spat his mum.

He shook his head like he was the disappointed parent and she the child. "Her name is Daizee. Now get out." His mum looked fiercely at him and he stared defiantly back at her refusing to give any ground. "For God's sake, get out and let her dress," he said more in disgust than anger. And to his surprise they did, or at least they got as far as the door to wait for him.

He turned to Daizee, "Ok?" he asked softly.

Daizee's head was bowed forward, she was breathing heavily holding her clothes to her chest. He could see tears on her cheeks. "I won't be long," he said. His parents backed off as he approached them, and shut the door behind him. He brushed passed his mum and dad without looking at them, down the corridor to his room, flicked the light switch, shut the door, crossed to his desk, picked up his school-sports hold-all, emptied it of school books, threw open drawers, pulled out clothes, tossed them into the bag, not caring for order or whether the pile of clothes remained folded and pressed. Stuffing the contents down he zipped the bag up, thought for a moment, stuffed his hand back into his bag, pulled everything out, found a pair of underpants, socks, t-shirt and jeans, and dressed. Then he stuffed everything back into the bag, zipped it shut, switched the light off, closed the door behind him, marched back down the corridor, passed his parents who were still frozen where he had left them. His mum called his name but he ignored her and carried on through to his dad's study.

"Come on," he said.

Daizee nodded.

"Where are you going?" said his mum behind him.

"I'm just going, mum," he said over his shoulder.

"It's the middle of the night," said his mum weakly.

"Lets go," he said to Daizee.

"When are you coming back?" demanded his mum.

He looked at her, her hair was wild from lying in bed, she looked insane. He shook his head.

"Ur coat," said Daizee softly.

"Francis?" cried his mum.

Without acknowledging his mum, Franky led Daizee out of the study into the hall to the enormous wardrobe, opened it, fished inside, found her coat, handed it to her, then took out his own.

"Francis?" said his dad still looking dazed.

Franky looked at his parents coldly, as if he was looking at them for the last time. Turning back to Daizee he said, "Let's go."

They did not slam the door, they shut it gently. When they got out into the street Franky's mum ran out and screamed his name. House lights flickered on, faces appeared in windows.

�
Act V

1

They walked in silence until they came to a park half a mile from where Franky lived. It was the darkest part of the night and there were no streetlights there, just moving shadows, but they went in anyway and took a place on a bench overlooking a wide green at the bottom of a hill. Daizee fished inside her coat pocket, took out her packet of cigarettes and, with a shaking hand, lit one. They sat in a state of wordless shock.

"I'm sorry," he said softly when she threw her finished cigarette away.

She nodded but didn't look at him.

"What shall we do?" he said after another long silence.

"Dunno."

"Shall we go back to your place?"

She shrugged her shoulders. "I suppose."

Still she refused to look at him. He stared at the side of her face and watched as the muscles of her jaw flexed. To draw some sort of reaction from her he said, "Or we could just go to the police," though he regretted saying it almost as soon as he mentioned it.

"Christ, Franky, don't start that again." She stared ahead at the park, biting her top lip.

"If we go to the police," he continued tentatively, "then we control what happens. Why would someone who's guilty hand themselves in? That just doesn't make sense."

"Nah, Franky, what don't make no sense ez ur handen

urselves in in the first place."

"Why not?"

"What fucken planet d'you live on?" she said.

He shook his head, looked hurt, turned away, thought for a moment then turned back. "You have to trust me on this –"

"What, like I trusted d'you with goen to yur folks? That worked out fucken well."

"Ok, that was stupid, but I thought it was the right thing to do."

"Like d'you fink goen to the cops ez a right fing to do?"

"This is different."

She turned on him. "Let I spell et out to d'you's, Franky. The reason why all this az appened ez cos I sucked Noel's dirty fucken cock, cos ur muh needed a fucken it of smack, then I tried to kill Noel an nicked iz drugs an cash. I thought I packed enough en iz works to kill a fucken field of orses, but the gear ee was peddlin was cut to shit. So now d'you know. If weez goes to the cops, Franky, thems gonna ask what that cunt was doen up thur with us. Even if us don't tell em nutten, thems gonna find out cos that's what them does. Thems'll ask about, in all the shit-oles that cunt ung about in. Noel's bound to ave said summut to some cunt or other, or thems'll find thur way to Cristol's. The point ez Franky d'you might be alright, sure fing thems'll believes d'you. D'you's come from ere, d'you's comes from fucken poshvilles, but I'z ez up to ur neck en shit. I stinks of et. D'you can't wash the smell off. Not d'you, not no one."

For a long time he looked at her, not knowing what to say to her, his eyes wide open with shock. She looked away from him afraid of what he might think of her, because just the thought of sucking Noel's cock made her feel disgusted so she could only imagine what he might feel, when he said,

"But Daizee, you're just a kid," which took her completely by surprise, especially when she looked at him and saw that his own face had become that of a little boy. She didn't want him feeling sorry for her. She blinked. "And d'your point ez?"

"They're supposed to look after you. That's what they do. That's what the law says they have to do."

She took out another cigarette, lit it, took in a huge, long drag of smoke, but didn't blow it out, instead she let it ooze from her nose and mouth. "When I was firteen I got hauled in by the cops, cos I was shacked up with some guy and iz mates. When I whirnt fucken im I was fucken them. Anyways, the cops auled them fellas in but let em go, didn't matter what I told em, the cops jus said 'Well what d'you's expect, d'you's a prostitute. Taint nutten weez can do for d'you's, ur love'."

"They didn't say that."

"Thems did and some. Thems said that I ad brought et on urself. That I ad led em on, which I might ave done, oo knowz."

"So what, you were thirteen. How old were these men?"

"Not ur age, that's for sure. Anyways, that's why I don't want to go to the cops. Thems'll jus dig out ur file and that's et, I'm banged to fucken rights an thems'll throw away the fucken key."

"You don't know that. Things have changed, Daizee."

"What, in two years? D'you fink?"

He felt his ears burn. "I don't know. Why not?"

"Look closer to ome Franky."

"What do you mean?"

"Yur muh, believes in God an all that, which sure enough I don't know nutten about, but I do know this, that et ez supposed to be all about love an that, tain I right?"

He nodded.

"Well she took one look at I an wanted to throw I out.

What jus appened, that was on the cards from the moment I'z walked into yur flat. Now, if that whir err reaction, what d'you fink some copper's gonna say when ee sees I? 'Fuck I, d'you been abused gurl, come on in weez gonna looks after d'you.' Nah Franky, taint the way of et." She breathed out a long shaft of smoke, which she finished with a smoke ring. "Weez so different."

"Are we?"

"Yes, Franky, weez are. Weez couldn't be more different. All this shit that az appened, this ez normal for I. Taint for d'you's. D'you might might fink d'you knowz about whir fings are in the whirld, but d'you taint got a fucken clue ow fings ez done, not really. The whirld taint fair, my beautiful Franky boy, not a fucken bit of et."

"I know that Daizee. I don't have to have lived it like you have. I can stand on the outside and watch it. I have read stuff. I do know a thing or two."

"That sounds like yur muh."

"I'm not like my mum," he snapped, "I'm here with you now, aren't I?

"No Franky, d'you's taint 'with I', d'you's can't be 'with I'. D'you's jus bin anging with I a little bit like dyou's on holiday or summut. An when all this is done d'you can go ome. So quit fucken about an go ome. Go back to yur muh. D'you can tell err about all an everfing that weez bin up to an she can old yur hand to the fucken cop shop."

She stood and threw her cigarette butt away.

"Where are you going?" he asked with panic in his voice.

"Ome. To bed."

"What about me?"

She breathed out. "D'you can come if d'you likes, but I taint goen to the cops."

"And if I did?"
"Then d'you's on yur own."

2

He watched her run and half walk to the top of the hill where, silhouetted by the damp glow of the streetlights, she slowed, hunched her shoulders then vanished down a street to the left. She didn't look back. He wanted her too, but knew that she wouldn't, which made what was happening all the more painful. He thought about running after her. Catching her up, stopping her by putting his hand on her shoulder like he had when she ran from him at the museum. But he didn't run after her. His body wouldn't let him.

She was right, in her world all this stuff was normal. He had no idea of the reality of it. He had fallen into her life. It was not the other way round. He was not meant to be there. But if he wasn't meant to be there, then what was he doing there standing in the cold with tears streaming down his face ?

"Francis Roberts," said a woman's voice behind him. He turned quickly to find two police officers standing there, a man and a woman.

"It's ok, Francis," said the woman, "your mum called us, you're not in any trouble. She was just worried that's all."

He took a step back. "I don't want to go home. I don't want to go back there."

The policewoman smiled. "It's ok Francis. Don't worry. You don't have to, if you don't want to." After a pause she added, "Where's Daizee?"

Something about the way she asked that question struck

him. They weren't there because his mum had called the police, or they might have been at first, but now that they had another thing on their minds.

He shook his head. "I don't know, she's gone." He breathed out, swallowed, felt his eyes flood and almost flow over. "I don't think she's going to come back."

The policewoman nodded. "You had an argument?"

"Not really. Not an argument." A tear escaped and rolled down his cheek.

"Hey," said the policewoman and she reached out and rubbed his shoulder, "it'll be alright."

The policeman watched with no expression on his face.

Franky shook his head. This time he couldn't stop the surge of tears, or prevent his shoulders from shaking uncontrollably. The police officers let him cry without saying anything. When he did finally collect himself the policewoman asked, "Which direction did she go in?"

He shrugged his shoulders, "I don't know, I didn't see. She just left." He pointed to his right, away from where Daizee had vanished. "That way. Down there."

The policewoman remained with him whilst her partner wandered off to speak into his radio.

"Francis, what happened between you and Daizee?"

"She just left," said Franky. He heard the voice on the other end of the police radio say, "We'll send a couple of cars, one for him and one to find the girl."

The policeman came back and nodded to his partner.

"Francis," said the woman, "we need you to come with us to the station."

Franky nodded. He started shaking. "Am I under arrest?"

"No, Francis."

"Call me Franky."

She nodded. "Ok. Franky"
"Someone did see us, didn't they?"
"See what?"
"At Cabot Tower?"
"What happened at Cabot Tower?"

Franky looked at her, then closed his eyes. When he opened them again he told her everything. Every detail. How they were up Cabot Tower looking at the view. How magical it had been. How perfect. How Noel had turned up with a knife wanting his drugs. How at first he was scared and couldn't move. How Daizee had kept it all together but had been forced to undress. How Noel had looked at her with this revolting desire in his eyes and at that moment she snatched the knife, and how he, Franky Roberts, had, in a blind and furious rage, thrown Noel to his death. How they had fled the scene. And how they didn't care about what they had done, because Noel had it coming, because of what he had done to her.

When he finished speaking Franky looked up at the sky. The sun was coming up, but he couldn't see it because of the clouds.

On the road above him a police car pulled up. He didn't wait to be told to move, he turned and made his way silently up the path towards it. The two police officers followed him. At the car he waited for them. The policewoman opened the door and he climbed in, then she got in beside him, shut the door and asked him to put his seatbelt on, which he did. The policeman got into the passenger seat in the front, nodded to the driver. His coat rustled loudly as he put his seatbelt on and without a word from any of them the car pulled away.

They drove up the hill in the direction that Daizee had gone and pulled into the road down which she had vanished. White blossom had fallen like snow on the pavement and Franky wondered whether she might have left some footprints, but there was nothing, not a single trace of her.